The Peace and Love collection

2020 The Forgotten Leap Year

By

Vendon Wright

Shield Crest

© Copyright 2022 Vendon Wright

All rights reserved.

ISBN: 978-1-913839-71-0

MMXXII

A CIP catalogue record for this book
is available from the British Library.

Published by
ShieldCrest Publishing,
Boston, Lincolnshire,
PE20 3BT England
Tel: +44 (0) 333 8000 890
www.shieldcrest.co.uk

Acknowledgements

Inspired by: Jessica Hotchkiss

Edited by: Chanel Mendez

Introduction

This book is one of several books based on the peace and love collection. Each of the books places the reader in difficult situations and then teaches people how to react correctly. The books include information on learning good morals and are full of humour and laughter.

Choices have consequences, so we need to help readers to make better ones. Sometimes they can't avoid getting into difficult situations but they can be taught how to react under pressure. These books will help facilitate learning. The journey towards adulthood involves many important life skills.

Each book takes the reader on a unique adventure, teaching them how to stay calm, having patience and key strengths on how to positively handle both stressful and difficult situations.

The books are considered as light reading, helping readers in learning new words and slowly building up their vocational skills to a much higher standard.

These multicultural books are both enjoyable to read and promote common sense from a young age.

Chapter 1

Lexie is a typical twelve-year-old female human. She has black wavy hair down to her shoulders and emerald green eyes. She attends a school in central London and has many friends.

There are only a few days left at school before they break up for Christmas. All the kids are very excited, but have a very strange way of showing it.

"It's break time," bellowed Lexie, "I need to meet my other friends outside."

"I'm coming too," said Nadia with a warm smile.

Nadia is Lexie's best friend. She has Brunette hair and hazel brown eyes. They were best friends back in first school and has always hung out together, refusing to let anyone else get between their friendship.

"Let's grab some snacks first."

They gathered their things together and rushed to the vending machine before procceding to meet the others.

They opened the school door and outside in the playground were several students all huddled up together. There was Helen, a short pretty blond, Lyn, a small Asian girl with silky black hair and Rachel and Rebecca, the twin girls with short brown hair. Most of the girls said hello to them but the boys remained quiet. Seamus, a stocky Irish kid looked over at Nadia and smiled before returning to concentrating on his mobile. Seamus has a thing for Nadia but has never told her. Nadia enjoys flirting with him and is waiting for the day he actually has a decent conversation with her, face to face and not through texting.

Lexie and Nadia approached Lyn.

"Hiya," said Lexie.

"Shhh," whispered Lyn, "be quiet, you don't want to upset any of the boys."

They quietly went behind her and found a comfortable space to stand. Lexie and Nadia reached into their bags and retrieved their mobile phones before logging onto an online game. Lexie held her mobile firmly in her left hand, Nadia tied back her hair in a hair band and then… there was silence. Nobody spoke, instead they all were playing a game or texting on their mobiles. You could hear a pin drop. Over thirty school children just stood there glued to their screens. The only sign of a conversation was through their mobiles. Every now and then you could hear a mobile vibrate as they proceeded to send each other messages. They were stood next to each other, sometimes even touching shoulders, but the only form of conversation was via text. They stood there in virtual silence, almost motionless apart from their tiny fingers vigorously tapping away.

After fifteen minutes the school bell rang to signal the end of break.

"That was fun," said Lexie.

"I think that I managed to get an almighty high score," replied Nadia.

Some students began to pass by them. Amongst them was Seamus and his friend Stephan.

"I think that I beat your high score Seamus," boasted Nadia.

"I already text you congratulations," answered Seamus in a strong Irish accent.

"Are you coming to class?" asked his friend Stephan.

"I'll be there now in a minute," answered Seamus.

"Stop flirting with the girls," teased Stephan.

"Go on will yah," returned Seamus.

"How are you Seamus?" asked Lexie.

"I'm grand."

"Your friend is waiting for you," commented Lexie.

"We can talk again tomorrow during morning break time," said Nadia addressing Seamus.

"You call that talking?" joked Lexie.

Just then, Nadia's mobile began to vibrate. Nadia looked down at her screen and chuckled. She had just received a text message from Seamus, who was standing just in front of her. He texted to confirm that he was looking forward to seeing her. Nadia text back to agree. Seamus then smiled at her and walked off with his friend Stephan.

"That was fun," said Nadia.

"Sorry, what did you say?" asked Lexie with a bewildered face on her.

"Seamus wants to meet me."

"What makes you say that?" asked Lexie.

"He text me a few moments ago, didn't you hear my mobile vibrate?"

"Sorry my mind must have drifted off."

They began to walk towards their next class.

"Did you see my almighty high score?" asked Nadia with excitement.

"You done well," replied Lexie.

"You are normally better than me at that game," remarked Nadia.

"I couldn't concentrate properly and my fingers felt a little numb."

Nadia turned her head to look down at Lexie's hand and then abruptly stopped. "Your hand looks swollen," she commented in a concerned tone.

"They do don't they."

Nadia gasped in sympathy. "And they look a little bumpy like you are developing spots or something."

"I don't know what's going on," said Lexie, "that's how they looked when I woke up this morning."

"Let's hope that you are not coming down with anything, it's Christmas in a few days and we have a lot of celebrating to do. Let's end 2019 with a bang."

Lexie gave Nadia a warm smile before entering their classroom.

After school, Lexie felt a little tired on the way home.

"Hi Lexie, how was school?" asked her mum as Lexie entered the house.

"Good but I feel tired."

"Well your food will be ready in a few minutes."

"I'll just go upstairs and get changed out of my school clothes first."

Lexie went to her room to get changed into her comfortable pyjamas before having something to eat down stairs with her family.

"Lexie, Lexie," a faint voice called.

Lexie slowly opened her eyes as the scene before her slowly became in focus. "Where am I?" she asked in a slurred tone.

"You are in hospital and I am Doctor Galliford."

"What, what happened?" asked Lexie in a more confused tone.

"Your parents couldn't wake you up, so they sent for an ambulance."

"Where are my parents?"

"They are just outside the door, I will call them in and let them know that you are awake."

The Doctor left the room and seconds later Lexie's parents entered.

"Thank God you are okay," bellowed her parents in unison.

"Why am I in hospital?"

"We called you for your dinner and you failed to answer," said mum.

"So I sent your mother up to your room," said dad.

"And you failed to respond to my calls, even when I shook you, so we called for an ambulance," commented mum.

"I would also like to send you for a CT scan," advised the Doctor.

There was silence for a moment while the Doctor wrote down a few notes.

"I feel sick," warned Lexie.

"Do you want me to take you to the bathroom?" asked her concerned mum.

Lexie paused while taking in a few deep breaths. "No, I think that I will be fine now."

A nurse left to quickly retrieve a small bed pan to collect any vomit.

"When was the last time you visited the bathroom?" asked the Doctor.

"I can't remember," replied Lexie.

"Have you visited the bathroom today?" asked the Doctor.

"No."

"How often do you visit the bathroom at school?"

"Sometimes once a day, sometimes I just don't feel like I need it."

The Doctor took more notes.

"I feel sick again," said Lexie now becoming quite frantic.

"Could you describe how you are feeling in more detail?" asked the Doctor.

"I feel like vomiting."

"I've got a pan for you to use if you like," said a kind Nurse.

"What's happening to my daughter?" asked Lexie's mum.

The Doctor wrote some more notes before responding. "I think that your daughter may have kidney failure."

"How is that possible?" asked her worried mum.

"Was it something I ate?" asked Lexie.

"It could happen to anyone, sometimes it happens very quickly."

"But she is so young," said mum.

"She is showing typical signs and symptoms, what we need to know is if it is acute or chronic kidney failure and what stage it maybe at."

"What do you mean what stage?" asked mum in a concerned tone.

"If it is stage five then she will need a kidney replacement."

Lexie's mum placed her hands against her mouth, almost too shocked to speak.

"What's happening?" asked Lexie who was totally baffled with the diagnosis.

"Could we have a second opinion from another Doctor?" asked mum.

"You are more than welcome to but we need to act quickly and the Radiologist department are always busy, so we need to book a CT scan now."

"I would like to consult another Doctor first," suggested mum.

Doctor Galliford left the room to find another Doctor.

Lexie's mum looked down and stared at her daughter, who was lying in the hospital bed looking quite weak.

"Everything is going to be okay," said her mum in a reassuring tone.

"Am I going to need a new kidney?"

"No dear, no, we will find a way to make you better."

"Why is this happening to me?"

Lexie's mum became emotional and began to cry.

After a short while a member of staff came around to ask if Lexie wanted anything to eat.

"No thanks, I don't feel hungry."

"What about some fruit," asked mum.

"I feel too tired to eat."

Then some Doctors came into the room. There were about five of them.

"I have brought a Doctor in to give you a second opinion," said Doctor Galliford.

"Hi Lexie, my name is Doctor Draper and these are some trainee doctors that have come to assist and diagnose what is wrong with you."

He asked mostly the same questions as Doctor Galliford and wrote down more notes.

"Have you got Diabetes?"

"No," replied Lexie.

"Is there any Diabetes in your family history?"

"No," interjected mum.

"Are you anaemic?"

"Why?"

"You are looking quite pale."

"My daughter isn't usually that pale," said mum.

Doctor Draper wrote down some more notes before responding. "I would like to send for some more tests and recommend an ultra sound."

"More tests," said mum.

"I'm tired of all these tests," commented Lexie.

Later on in the evening, some nurses came in and wheeled Lexie out to have her ultra sound. Her mum stayed by her side during her tests.

"That's it, all finished," said one nurse as they wheeled her back into her room.

"What about the CT scan?" asked mum.

"We can't fit her in until Boxing day," replied Doctor Draper, who had now re-joined them in the room."

"What! am I going to be in hospital for Christmas?" asked Lexie in a frantic rage.

"Yes," answered Doctor Draper.

"Can't she come home with us and then we just bring her back on Boxing day?" mum pleaded.

"I'm afraid not, she is far too ill and weak to leave the hospital."

"My Christmas is ruined," cried Lexie, now with tears streaming down her face.

"How did she get to stage 5 kidney failure so quickly?" asked mum.

"Chronic Kidney disease can appear quite rapidly, sometimes showing little signs and symptoms."

"How long has she got to live?"

"She has End stage kidney failure, so needs dialysis or kidney replacement as soon as possible."

"Merry Christmas and Happy New year to me," cried Lexie while tears fell from her puffed out eyes.

Her mum gave her a comforting warm hug before continuing. "What do you recommend?" she asked.

"She will either have to go for regular dialysis or have a kidney transplant."

"Which one do you recommend Doctor?" asked mum.

"Dialysis which will make her weak, unless someone comes with a kidney replacement."

"How likely is she to have a kidney replacement?"

"Over New Year, highly unlikely, unless you believe in miracles."

Lexie's mum looked towards her crying daughter and paused with thought.

"We recommend her start dialysis straight away," suggested Doctor Galliford.

"Could we leave it a few days to decide?"

"Why would you want to delay?" asked Doctor Draper.

"We would like to go home and pray on it," replied mum.

"Lexie has become too weak and will need to stay in hospital over New Year," advised Doctor Draper.

"So I can't even take my little girl home?"

All the Doctors remained silent.

The next few days passed quickly. Lexie's family had come into the hospital on New Year's eve to celebrate New Year with her, but in the evening they were asked to leave the hospital. Before they left, mum asked her to pray at midnight and they too would be praying for her at home, at the same time.

First thing in the morning on New Year's day, several Doctors rushed into Lexie's room.

"We have some fantastic news for you," said Doctor Draper.

Lexie gave them a tired look but remained silent.

"We have found a donor and we have a kidney for you."

Lexie sat up bolt upright and smiled. "How were you able to find one so quickly?"

"It just came in this morning unexpectedly."

"Who from?"

"Apparently they want to remain anonymous."

"But why?"

"We don't know, but we have tested it early this morning and it is a perfect match."

"So what now?" asked Lexie now with a slight sound of excitement in her voice.

"She can't manage see," said mum.

Paula turned to face Lexie. "Okay, you little brat," she retorted in a huff.

"And make me some food," added Lexie, now with a dirty great big grin on her face.

Paula rolled her eyes, then turned and went to the kitchen to make food in a huff, while Lexie sat there texting her friends.

At the start of new term, Lexie returned to school and she was very excited to actually see her friends in person.

"Nadia," bellowed Lexie.

"Lexie, you're back," replied Nadia now turning to give her a big hug.

"I missed you guys."

"I better not squeeze you too tight, I wouldn't want to hurt you," said Nadia in a concerned tone.

"Nothing wrong with me now," said Lexie with a big warm smile on her face.

"Lexie," another voice shouted.

She turned to see her friend Lyn running towards them.

Lexie was the new talk of the school and soon other friends gathered around her.

"Hi Rachel and Hi Rebecca," said Lexie.

"No, I'm Rebecca and that's Rachel," remarked Rebecca.

Lexie looked with a blank face towards them.

"Has it been that long that you have forgotten which twin we are?" added Rachel.

They all began to giggle.

"Group hug," suggested Nadia.

They hugged each other and welcomed Lexie back.

Other friends crowded around Lexie at the start of their first class, asking all sorts of questions. The girls spoke face to face, but the boys were too shy so resorted to texting her.

"You missed all the fun and games we had on the last day of term," said Rebecca, one of the twins.

"I was in hospital for Christmas and New Year," said Lexie.

"Did you really have a new kidney?" asked Nadia.

"Yes."

"Did it hurt?" asked Rebecca.

"No."

"Wow," they all murmured.

"You're so brave," said Rachel, the other twin.

"You missed all the food and drinks we had on our Christmas party," informed Lyn.

"I didn't eat anything for Christmas in hospital."

"How did you survive??" asked Rachel.

"They had to feed me intravenously."

"Wow," they all murmured, not really knowing what that even meant.

Some more students walked in and joined into the conversation.

"You're back," screamed Helen a timid blond, "are you still in any pain?"

"No, nothing."

"Are you sure it didn't hurt?" asked Rebecca.

"No, I didn't feel a thing," replied Lexie with a joyful smile.

Rachel just looked over with piercing wide eyes.

"How long were you under the knife?" asked Nadia.

"Two or three hours."

"Have you got any scarring?" asked Helen.

"Nothing."

"So you have someone else's kidney inside you?" asked Rebecca.

"Yep."

"Wow," they all murmured.

"Do you know who donated the kidney?" asked Helen.

"No, apparently she wanted to remain anonymous."

"At least you got it from a girl, imagine if you had a boys kidney inside you," commented Nadia.

They all giggled joyfully.

"Doesn't it feel strange having someone else's kidney inside?" asked Rachel.

"No, but something strange did happen," replied Lexie now with a serious face on her.

"What? Tell us more," demanded Rebecca.

"When I awoke, someone else was in my room."

"What do you mean?" asked Rachel.

"There was a little girl just staring down at me with big blue eyes."

"Was she lost?" asked Nadia.

"I was on my own in a separate room."

"Are you sure?" asked Rebecca.

"Well that's what the Doctor said when he walked in seconds later."

"Maybe she left quickly," remarked Rachel.

"Maybe," Lexie agreed hesitantly.

"What did she look like?" asked Lyn.

"It was very blurred when I woke up, but I think that she had blond hair and big blue eyes."

"Did she say anything to you?" asked Nadia.

"She said something about I am healed."

"Then what?" asked Nadia.

"Then she just vanished, disappeared right before my eyes."

"Wow," they murmured.

Rachel gave a disbelieving look and then turned away.

The school bell rang and the Teacher walked in.

"Morning class, my name is Mr Knott, I will be teaching you maths."

Mr Knott began to throw out a few maths questions and tested how quickly the students worked out the answers. Lexie felt the finally resorted to looking up a complicated question from a text book. He flicked through some pages and then paused. The moment had come when he made his choice and directed it towards her. She sat in silence for a few seconds giving the impression that she did not know the answer.

"Okay class, I am handing out an exam test which none of you should be able to complete. We will then calculate from the highest marks to see what result you all would have received."

Just then, Violet announced her answer.

"Have you really been sitting there working that out?" asked the Teacher.

"Yes Sir."

"Did she manage to get it right?" asked Helen.

The Mr Knott paused with embarrassment. "Yes," he replied.

The class gave her a round of applause.

After the lesson had finished, Lexie and her friend Nadia decided to stay behind and confront Violet. They approached her just outside the classroom door.

"Hi," said Lexie.

Violet looked straight towards her and gave her a warm smile.

"Hi," replied Violet.

"You were amazing at answering those questions," encouraged Nadia.

"That's because they were easy," replied Violet.

"How could you find the questions easy when the whole class struggled?" asked Nadia.

"I memorise everything."

"Our little minds are not big enough to memorise everything," added Lexie.

"You would be surprised with the capacity of your brain," commented Violet.

"Why did you delay answering the last question?" asked Nadia.

"Now that's a little secret," Violet replied with a cheeky smile.

"Sorry to be rude," interrupted Lexie, "our names are;"

"I already know your names, Lexie and Nadia, yes?"

"And your name is Violet," returned Lexie.

The girls giggled, while Nadia wore a puzzled expression across her face.

Then Lexie got straight to the point. "Sorry to ask but have we met before?"

"No," replied Violet.

"Who?" asked Nadia.

"It's just that you look remarkably like a girl I met in hospital."

"Why were you in hospital?"

"I had a kidney transplant."

"When?"

"A week ago."

"How are you back in school so quickly?"

"The Doctor said that I was heeled and well enough to return to normality."

"You are so strong," said Violet.

Lexie stared towards her with suspicion. "Are you sure we haven't met before?" she asked.

"No, sorry you must be confusing me with someone else."

The girls stood looking at each other for a moment.

"Would you like to hang with us outside?" asked Lexie.

"Sure."

"Let's go outside and join the others," said Nadia in confusion.

"Why?" inquired Violet.

"We all get together and play on our mobiles," said Lexie.

"Well I will give it a try."

They walked out of the school door onto the playground and joined the others.

"Now what?" asked Violet.

"Now you play online games or text people on your mobile," answered Lexie.

Immediately Lexie's mobile pinged.

"Why did that boy send you a message when you are just a few meters away from him?" asked Violet.

"That's how we speak."

"Don't you kids communicate verbally anymore?"

"The girls do, but the boys don't," replied Lexie.

"Are the boys shy, or… dumb?"

Lexie chuckled.

"What are you laughing at?" asked Nadia worryingly.

"Boys are not very good at communicating or having a decent conversation."

Then Violet turned her head quickly to look towards the twins. "That girl with the short brown hair just text something nasty about you," she said.

"They are Rachel and Rebecca the twins, so which one?" enquired Lexie.

"The one on the left."

"That's Rachel, wait a moment, you surely can't see her mobile phone screen from here, so how do you know?"

"That's another little secret," replied Violet.

They stood thinking for a while.

"What did she text?" asked Lexie.

"Who?" asked Nadia.

"I'll show you," said Violet.

Violet looked at her mobile which was in the palm of her left hand and called the name Lexie, while flexing her right arm out straight to catch an incoming mobile. In an instant, just like magic, Rachel's mobile flew out of her hand and landed in the palm of Lexie's right hand.

"Here, read it for yourself," said Violet.

Lexie and Violet giggled to themselves for a second.

"How did you do that?" asked Nadia.

"Cool trick, right," answered Violet.

At the same time, Rachel quickly became aware that she had just lost her mobile and was frantically searching around for its whereabouts.

Chapter 6

"That was amazing," said Lexie while they walked off towards their next class.

"How did you make Rachel do everything you commanded?" asked Nadia.

"I'm just very persuasive," replied Violet.

"Have you got mind control or something?" asked Nadia.

"Maybe," replied Violet as she and Lexie began to laugh.

"What's with that cool mobile?" asked Lexie, "and why does it light up like a Christmas tree?"

"It's a special mobile," replied Violet.

"Why's it called Lexie?" asked Lexie.

"You're Lexie," interjected Nadia.

"It's new technology," replied Violet.

"What do you mean?" asked Nadia who was now wearing a baffled expression across her face.

"It's the upgraded version of your Googla."

"So you can command it to do things?" asked Lexie.

"Yes."

"Like getting students to do fun things," added Lexie.

"Who's having fun?" asked Nadia just as they entered their classroom.

The next day at school, Rachel did her best to avoid Lexie, still suffering from embarrassment from the previous day. Her twin sister Rebecca occasionally spoke but mostly remained loyal to her sister. Nobody knew why Rachel would choose to crouch down and crawl. Some girls like Lyn and Helen asked a few questions, but the boys resorted to send both Lexie and Nadia text messages concerning the subject.

"I just had a funny text message from Francisco," said Lexie joyfully.

"I just received another text message from Seamus," said Nadia.

"What did it say?" asked Lexie.

"He wants to know if you put a spell on her."

"Maybe Violet but not me," replied Lexie

"What do you mean?" asked Nadia.

"I was just playing a mind game on her," said Violet.

"You know that she is conspiring to get you back," warned Nadia.

"How do you know that?" asked Lexie.

"Just a rumour I heard," said Nadia.

"I'm not scared," replied Violet with a slight chuckle.

"Why do you keep laughing to yourself?" asked Nadia.

Time seemed to be speeding up. Something just didn't feel normal in the air and Violet became a little restless.

"I need to go somewhere urgently," said Violet.

"You are in school so you can't leave," said Lexie.

"I'm not going anywhere," said Nadia.

"I'll be back before break," said Violet and she left the classroom without asking the Teacher for leave.

Lexie felt abandoned without her, Violet was her new best friend. Lexie didn't care if she was the girl from the hospital or not, she just felt more secure and protected having her new friend Violet always at her side.

It was break time again. Nadia and Lexie walked outside and joined the crowd of students already playing on their mobiles. A few students took a quick glance at them before resuming their online games. Lexie looked around and noticed that the twins were missing.

"Well at least I don't have to confront Rachel on my own," said Lexie.

"What do you mean on your own?" asked Nadia while she finished tying her hair back.

"I feel more confident having Violet around."

Just then Violet appeared. "I'm back," she said.

"You scared me," said Lexie frantically.

"Who scared you?" asked Nadia.

"Sorry, I did say that I wouldn't abandon you," said Violet.

"Did you just appear out of thin air or something?" asked Lexie.

"I haven't been anywhere," said Nadia in confusion.

Violet just laughed.

"What's so funny?" asked Nadia.

"Nobody's talking again," said Violet.

"That's what kids do," said Lexie.

"Who?" asked Nadia.

"Not anymore," said Violet, "it's time they all learnt to communicate with each other."

Violet opened her left palm to reveal her mobile and called the name Lexie. Her mobile began to light up like a Christmas tree. It had all the colours of the rainbow flashing beautiful combinations of colours. Violet mumbled something and all the other mobiles in the school playground began to vibrate. There was silence for a split second before everyone frantically looked around at each other.

"What have you done?" asked Lexie.

"Who are you talking to?" asked Nadia.

"See how they manage without a mobile for a while," replied Violet with a triumphant smile beaming across her face.

"My mobile has just gone dead," said Lexie.

"My mobile has gone dead too," said Nadia while looking down at her blank screen.

"So has mine," said Seamus who had decided to come over with his friend Stephan.

"What are we going to do?" asked Nadia in a huff, now pressing keys on her mobile at random.

"Have a conversation with each other," suggested Violet.

"I think that the electric grid has gone down," commented Max who had just walked over to join them.

"What do you mean?" asked Seamus.

"That's where we get all our electric from to run the school," replied Max.

"You don't know what you does be saying," commented Seamus in a strong Irish accent.

More students came over questioning them.

"What just happened?" asked Helen in a timid voice.

"I don't know," answered Lexie.

"I have disconnected all your mobile services," said Violet.

"All our mobiles are no longer working," said Lyn, "It's like all our batteries have lost power."

"I told you," insisted Max, "the electric grid has gone down."

"I heard an Emp ray can knock all electrical devices within a fifty metre radius," commented Helen softly.

"What do you mean?" asked Seamus.

"It's an electromagnetic pulse," replied Helen.

"My dad says he works with Hydroelectric power with those capabilities," commented Max.

"What are you going on about?" asked Seamus.

"They would need an extremely large power source to knock out all of our electrical devices," answered Max.

"But all the lights are still on in school," remarked Lyn.

They all looked towards the school and then back towards Max for a response.

"Well, that's what my dad said," remarked Max in a raised tone.

"Now you know why they call him mad Max," commented Stephan.

Some students began to giggle cheerfully.

The conversation went on.

"At least the boys are actually trying to have a conversation with the girls now," commented Violet.

"Maybe it's the 5G that they are all installing to speed up our mobile services," said Seamus.

"My mobile is 4G," said Stephan.

"Let Seamus continue," interjected Helen.

"They are setting up 5G towers to kill us with radiation," continued Seamus.

"You what?" remarked Helen, "I stopped Stephan from speaking to hear you invent that rubbish."

"It's true," insisted Seamus, "they are lying, they are using smoke and mirrors to hide what is really going on."

"Nobody's trying to kill us," remarked Helen, "you sound as crazy and mad as Max."

"I heard that," bellowed Max.

Students chuckled.

"What else could have happened?" asked Nadia.

"Does anyone have a valid theory of what is actually going on?" asked Debbie now trying to get in on the conversation.

"Maybe someone has hacked our main frame," suggested Seamus, "using special spyware software."

"What about an alien invasion," invented mad Max, "maybe the spaceships are cloaked and sitting just outside our atmosphere."

Lexie rolled her eyes and sighed, knowing that it was only Violet playing a game with them all.

"You are crazy Max," said Stephan.

"No I'm not," shouted Max pushing Stephan back with his hands in a mad rage.

"Okay, calm down boys," interjected Lexie, "we are just having some fun with you."

"How can we have fun without our mobiles?" asked Helen weakly.

"Try having a sensible conversation," suggested Violet.

"We could try and change the subject from talking about aliens," joked Nadia.

Max stared towards her with his chest puffed out ready to defend himself again.

Maybe it's a loss of AM and FM radio signal that interferes with our radio waves of our mobiles," suggested Debbie.

"Caused by an electric storm," added Max.

"Or lightning," said Seamus.

"Or a Meteor shower," invented Max.

They all looked towards Max with blank expressions on their faces.

"Where are you going with this now Max?" asked Stephan.

"It could have come from a Red giant, yellow giant or supernova," continued Max.

"What about Black holes?" asked Debbie.

Everyone turned their heads and looked towards Debbie.

"There are Lots of planets in our Galaxy, not just nine," remarked Max.

Students then turned their heads towards Max with their mouths open.

"I saw it on a game," interrupted Debbie.

Students quickly turned their heads back in amazement to face Debbie.

"These kids sure make up stories fast," giggled Violet.

"I expected more from you Debbie," Nadia responded sternly.

"These kids sure have convoluted conspiracy theories," concluded Lexie.

The school bell sounded and students returned inside

"I now feel overwhelmed with information," chuckled Violet.

"Me too," laughed Lexie.

"What are you laughing at?" asked Nadia.

"Nothing," replied Lexie as she watched Violet open her left hand and mumble something to her colourful flashing mobile in her left palm.

All the services were then restored back to their mobiles.

"I've got to rush off again," bellowed Violet as she prepared to disappear once again.

"What about class?" asked Lexie.

"I'll meet you later," replied Violet and she was gone.

"Lexie, where are you going?" asked Nadia in confusion.

Chapter 7

Over the next few weeks, Lexie and Violet's friendship became even closer. Lexie was hanging around with and calling Violet on her mobile more than her best friend Nadia.

"Where do you keep running off to?" asked Lexie.

"I have important places to be," replied Violet.

"Like where?"

"Like saving the world," giggled Violet.

"It's not like you need to be in school anyway, I still can't believe you scored 100% in that maths test at the beginning of term."

"I just find maths easy."

"Everyone else seems to struggle."

"You score well these days."

"It's strange, but sometimes the answers just come to me," said Lexie.

"Trust your mind," encouraged Violet, "your mind is capable of storing much more information than you have been told."

Just then, Lexie's mum called for her to join them downstairs for dinner.

"I've got to go."

"I've got places to be anyway."

"You've been promising to come over and meet my family."

"Soon," replied Violet and she was gone.

"Your food is getting cold," said Lexie's mum just as Lexie took a seat at the dinner table.

"Sorry, I was on my phone speaking to my friend Violet."

Lexie served herself some food and began to tuck in.

"Who is this friend Violet that you keep on talking about?" asked her sister Paula.

"She's my best friend at school."

"I thought that Nadia was your best friend?" asked dad.

"Can't I have two best friends?"

"We have yet to meet her," said mum.

"I thought you kids just text each other," remarked Paula.

"No, that's the boys, us girls know how to have a conversation."

"What do you talk about for so long," asked mum.

"Aliens taking over the planet," replied Lexie with a slight chuckle.

"What do you mean?" asked Paula.

"The boys at my school still think that there are Aliens controlling us from space."

"You are not still talking about the day you lost service on your mobile, are you?" asked mum.

"Yes."

"That could quite easily be explained," said Paula.

"Up and down the Country," replied Derek.

They all looked around at each other with baffled expressions radiating across their faces.

There was a knock at the front door.

"Would you kindly get that please honey?" asked Caroline.

Lexie and Paula continued to sit in silence eating, while their dad got up and went to open the front door.

"Hello Sir, please could we come in?"

"What's happened?" asked Derek hesitantly.

"It's nothing serious, we would just like to have a word with your daughter Lexie Amber Brooke."

"What's she done?"

"Please could we come in and have a word with her, or would you prefer to do it down at the Police Station?"

Derek let them in and led the Officers through to the dining room.

"There are two Policemen here to have a word with Lexie," said Derek entering the room.

Caroline clapped her hand against her mouth in sheer surprise.

"What has she done?" asked Paula.

"That's what we are here to find out."

The Officers turned their attention to Lexie. "Is your name Lexie Amber Brooke?"

"Yes," replied Lexie lifting her head up from eating.

They stared directly towards Lexie.

"Where were you at 2pm on Friday 12th February?"

"At school," replied Lexie nervously.

"Why?" asked her dad Derek.

"Someone with her description was spotted outside a bank speaking to some bank robbers."

"What!" screamed Caroline now in a frantic shock.

"But she was at school," commented dad.

"Did you leave your school early at any time that day?"

Lexie thought for a moment before responding.

"No, I left school with my friend Violet at 3.30pm normal time."

"What's happened?" asked mum.

"Someone robbed the bank at around that time."

And you think that it was our Lexie?" mum frantically asked.

"No."

"Then why are you here frightening our daughter?" asked dad.

"We would like to know what she spoke to the robbers about."

They all stared towards Lexie for a response.

"I was in school all day," Lexie defended, "I was mum."

"Someone of her description was caught on camera speaking to the robbers."

"Well it wasn't me," replied Lexie in fury.

There was silence for a split second.

"Are you here to arrest her?" asked dad.

"No."

"Then why are you here?" mum asked with a puzzled expression.

"We would like to know what she said to the robbers to convince them to hand themselves in."

Chapter 8

It was Friday 28th February. Lexie had returned from school with her friend Violet and invited her in for dinner with her family.

"I can't come in," said Violet.

"Why not? You have let me down every time I invite you in and my parents still think that you are a figment of my imagination."

"I just can't, not yet."

They stood in perfect view so that Lexie's parents could see them from the lounge window.

"Why can't you just pop in for a quick minute just to say hello to my parents to settle their minds?" Lexie begged.

"Maybe later," replied Violet.

Lexie's front door opened and her father looked towards them.

"Will you ring me later?"

"Lexie Amber Brooke, who are you speaking to?" asked dad.

Lexie turned her head to look over her shoulder. "Hi dad, this is my friend Violet."

There was a gentle breeze that made Lexie's hair slightly sway. Lexie turned back to face Violet, but there was nobody there.

"Where has she gone?" asked Lexie frantically.

"Who?" asked dad.

"My friend Violet was just standing speaking to me."

"I saw you from the lounge window and you were standing there alone."

"That's impossible," bellowed Lexie who was glancing around in search of Violet's whereabouts.

"Come inside dear and we will talk."

Lexie went in with her dad and he closed the front door.

"We need to talk," said dad while pacing up and down the lounge and awaiting assistance from his wife.

Lexie slammed her school bag down on the floor and grumpily sat on the sofa with her arms crossed.

"Why were you stood outside the front gate?" asked mum entering the room.

"I was speaking to Violet."

"Hunny, you were standing there alone," said mum.

"She was there but she didn't want to come in."

"I suppose she just disappeared," remarked dad.

"I haven't made her up, she is real."

"You are having paranoid delusions," said dad.

"I haven't invented her, she is real," bellowed Lexie.

"Those brain butchers at the hospital messed with your mind," commented mum.

"I had surgery on my kidney not my brain mum," remarked Lexie cheaply.

"Well, you were standing outside on your own, speaking to yourself," said mum.

"I was speaking to Violet."

"You never saw her, it was a hallucination," ordered dad.

Lexie sighed and sat in a huff.

"Have you hit your head?" asked mum

"Why?"

"Maybe you have amnesia," suggested mum.

"That's a loss of memory," replied Lexie sarcastically.

"Where is this Violet then?" continued mum.

"I don't know where she has gone, but she's got this angelic personality that you would love when you finally meet her."

"We need definitive proof that she exists," said dad.

"Then I will just have to go and find her."

Lexie hastily sprang to her feet and prepared to leave the room.

"Where are you going young lady??" dad asked sternly.

"To my room."

"You haven't eaten any dinner," said mum.

"I'm not hungry anymore."

With that Lexie ran upstairs, flung herself onto her bed and sobbed.

During the night, Lexie felt restless, unable to settle and not having much luck going to sleep. It might have been from having an empty stomach, but she also had a lot on her mind. Had she been hallucinating? Was she delusional? Was Violet manifested from having an active imagination? Lexie lay there deep in thought and then finally came to the conclusion that she was seeing Violet in her head, so she began to cry, thinking that she was slowly going mad.

Then, almost out of nowhere came a voice.

"Lexie, Lexie," a faint voice called.

Lexie slowly opened her eyes as the scene before her slowly became more focussed.

"Where am I?" asked Lexie in a slurred, tired tone.

"You are in your bedroom and I am your friend Violet."

"You're just a delusion, a voice in my head," said Lexie.

"I'm over here."

Lexie looked over towards her mirror and saw nothing out of the ordinary in her dim lit room.

"My dad said that you are not real and I have manifested Violet in my mind."

"Come over to the mirror," the voice ordered.

Lexie got up, grabbed her mobile phone to use its light and slowly walked closer.

"Now look in the mirror," Violet's voice demanded.

Lexie peered into the mirror and saw a reflection of herself.

"See, you are just a voice in my head."

"Look closer and you will see me."

Lexie looked harder at her reflection and just stared for a moment.

"Surprise," said Violet.

Now Lexie noticed that even though the image in the mirror appeared to look identical to her reflection, it was not, for now her mouth was moving and speaking, but not synchronised to what Lexie was saying. It was spooky to watch herself speaking back in the mirror.

"How are you?" asked Violet.

A cold shiver ran down her spine. "I don't understand, how are you doing that?" asked Lexie

"I am a Clone replicate of you."

"How did you get in the mirror?"

"I am from another dimension."

"Like a phantom zone?" asked Lexie.

"Yes."

"Are you here to hurt me?"

"No, I came through the portal opened back in January."

"How?"

"2020 is a special leap year."

"Why?" asked Lexie now becoming a little uneasy.

"Because there are two days added to February this year."

Lexie started to freak out.

"It is not mathematically possible," commented Lexic.

"Your scientists know that there are not actually 365 and a quarter days in a year, so every 400years time becomes misaligned and opens a portal to correct itself."

Lexie paused, brushing her hair back with her hands, but her image in the mirror just smiled back at her.

"Why are you here?" asked Lexie.

"We are a doomed race and scientists say we will practically not exist in about 50 years."

"Why do you look like me?"

"I borrowed piece of your DNA."

"So, you can replicate us?"

"In the future, yes."

"Are you an alien entity?"

"No, I am a prototype human."

"All that from a little piece of our DNA?" asked Lexie inquiringly.

"They don't just borrow your DNA, I also have all your thoughts and all your memories."

"So, you are a carbon copy, my doppelganger?"

"Yes, they made me into the perfect clone," said the image now with an even bigger smile reflecting back through the mirror at Lexie.

They stared at each other for a moment, with Lexie becoming more baffled. "How did you have blonde hair before but now you look just like me?"

"We are shape shifters and can take on any image."

"So where is the blonde Violet?"

"Here I am."

With that Violet transformed before Lexie's face, almost like a jigsaw puzzle reassembling its pieces. Lexie looked into the mirror at her reflection and then saw...Violet staring back at her.

"How is this possible?" asked Lexie.

"They took some cells from your body, DNA Produced from a single ancestry. My cells can regenerate and that's how I am able to take on different appearances."

"And you also took all my memories?" asked Lexie.

"They uploaded identical information and memories and expanded your brains capacity. Your Cerebral capacity is about 10% for humans and 5% for animals, but they have unlocked parts of the brain so I am now using about 70%. You could say that I am genetically advanced."

Lexie just stared at her image in the mirror which was now reflecting a teenage girl with blonde hair tied in a French plait, smiling proudly back at her.

Time went on and it was now seconds before midnight and the beginning of the two day Leap Year.

"I'm not just a voice in your head. We have now unlocked the secret of transforming matter," said Violet.

Lexie focussed on Violet in the mirror with worry and confusion. "What do you mean?"

"At the stroke of midnight, I will be able to transport from my dimension into yours."

"Do you mean time travel?"

"Yes."

Lexie looked over to her clock on the bedroom wall and nervously watched as the seconds counted down. At the stroke of midnight, there was a warm light that surrounded Lexie. The room was then filled with a bright glow that slowly dissipated. Lexie's hair blew in the brisk breeze just as Violet materialized before her face.

Chapter 9

Lexie stepped forward and found herself in another town, not realising that she was just part of a magical transportation.

"Wait, what just happened?" asked Lexie observing her surroundings and wondering where her bedroom had suddenly disappeared to.

Violet released her grip from Lexie's hand and just smiled back at her for a moment.

"You have just experienced your first teleportation."

"Wait, what?"

"I turn in the direction I want to go in and then release myself from your gravity, then I automatically get teleported somewhere else."

"Holy, moly," remarked Lexie in sheer surprise.

"Gravity is temporally deactivated and it allows us to travel using Laser technology. Then we use electromagnetic stabilisers to reconnect to the Magnetic fields of Earth."

Lexie didn't quite understand a word Violet was saying.

"So you are saying that I can fly?"

"Well, technically I was doing the flying, but yes," replied Violet jokingly.

"Holy moly, I can fly," screamed Lexie with excitement.

Lexie fixed her hair that had become a slight mess from the transportation and then glanced at her mobile which showed they had just taken a few seconds to reach their destination.

"How fast were we travelling?"

"I have multiple speed capabilities, but I would say Warp speed because I just trust the force the Earth's magnetic field enhances."

"So… are you a Jedi?"

Violet giggled.

Violet looked around using her mobile's echo location abilities.

"Where are we?" asked Lexie.

"Manchester."

"Holy moly, one minute we are in London the next we are in Manchester," Lexie bellowed.

"The people we are looking for are in that direction," pointed Violet.

"How do you know that?" enquired Lexie.

"I can sense their heat signatures that is connected to their life force."

"Sense who?"

"The people robbing the jewellery store."

"Why does that matter to us?"

"Everything we do affects the future of the human race. There will be lots of looting unless we learn to love one another, so we need to unite together to survive and promote peace around the world."

Lexie looked in the direction of the criminals.

"So, what now?"

"Time for me to change into my combat gear."

With that, Violet spoke to her mobile, which then lit up flashing with brilliantly coloured lights in her left hand and Lexie stood there and witnessed her Metaphysical transformation.

"You look like me again."

Violet now had long black hair and green eyes.

"Yes, but at least I am not in my pyjamas," Violet chuckled.

Lexie took a quick glance at herself and almost screamed.

"What! You removed me from my bedroom in my pyjamas?"

"Sorry, we didn't have time to change."

"Well, you just did," returned Lexie in embarrassment.

Lexie straitened herself to try and look more presentable.

"Lucky I was wearing my Queen-B girls run the world pyjamas."

Violet chuckled some more.

They carefully walked closer to the door of the Jewellery store and looked through the window to witness the siege. Outside were two unarmed policemen awaiting backup.

"Can you twins please stay back out of harm's way," advised one of the officers.

"You stay here, I'm going in," whispered Violet into Lexie's ear.

"Are you mad?" muttered Lexie.

"I am immortal so cannot get hurt, but you are mortal so stay here."

Violet took a quick glance back through the window and almost looked as though she was staring through the walls inside to determine the threat.

"This won't take long."

With that, Violet began her walk towards the door.

"Where do you think you are going?" screamed one of the officers.

"I think that my dad is in there so I am going in to save him."

Violet opened the door with her hands raised high into the air and her mobile began to glow a brilliant shade of violet.

"Get out of here little girl before you get hurt," ordered one of the criminals.

Violet stared into his eyes, blinked and then smiled.

"You don't want to hurt anyone do you?" asked Violet.

There was a slight pause.

"I don't want to hurt anyone," said the one standing directly in front of her.

"Put down the gun," ordered Violet.

The man immediately dropped the gun to the ground.

"Why did I do that? I didn't want to do that," muttered the confused criminal.

"Now go outside like a good little boy and give yourself into the nice Police officers outside."

He turned almost on command and walked out.

Another criminal pointed his gun at Violet.

"What did you say to him?"

"I don't know but something deadly has managed to come through the portal, and I really need to leave now."

"Can't you stay until the morning to meet my parents?"

"No."

Lexie looked down at her bedroom floor in disappointment.

"You have to stay," Lexie demanded, "my parents still think that you are a figment of my imagination."

"Shhh, keep it down or you might wake them up."

"At least they would come in and see that you are real," replied Lexie in a slight huff.

"Okay, okay, I will come back and meet them first thing in the morning."

"No, don't leave me, that's what you said last time."

"I won't let you down this time, here, you can have my special belt as proof that I am real."

They both stood up. Violet removed her chunky shiny black, silver and violet belt from around her waist and placed it firmly around Lexie.

"What's so special about this belt," asked Lexie whilst admiring its beauty.

"This belt, it renders the wearer immortal."

Chapter 10

L exie was eating her breakfast and already the questioning began from her parents.

"I thought that your friend Violet was joining us for breakfast this morning?" asked dad.

"She will turn up, she promised me," returned Lexie.

"You have been talking about her for weeks and she still has not made an entrance," said mum.

"I still think that it is all in her head," said dad.

"She's real, you will see," replied Lexie.

With that, Lexie put her hand firmly onto her new belt and remembered that it was Violet's gift to her.

"Look at this belt," said Lexie now standing up, "Violet gave it to me."

Her parents stared towards the shiny black leather belt.

"Where did you get that from?" asked mum who was slowly becoming suspicious.

"I told you, Violet gave it to me," answered Lexie.

Lexie's mum calmly approached and took a closer look at the leather belt.

"This can't be real," gasped mum, "are those gemstones studded all around it in the shape of flowers? And what is this, a crystal parrot?"

"That must be precious," added dad admiring its beauty, "who would give such an expensive gift away?"

"Keep it down please girls," the Teacher said, ushering them to be quiet in the library.

A short while later, Rachel and Rebecca entered the library. Rachel gave a dirty look towards Lexie and then slowly approached her.

"Oh God, troubles approaching," said Nadia.

"I hear you have been talking about me," Rachel complained.

"What have I done wrong now?" asked Lexie.

"I don't know how but you tried to make a fool of me a few weeks ago and now that it's the last day of school, it's time for me to get my own back."

Violet's voice entered Lexie's head.

"Would you like me to knock her out?" Violet asked telepathically.

"No," screamed Lexie.

"What do you mean no?" asked Rachel.

"I wasn't talking to you," answered Lexie glancing from Rachel towards Violet, who was just sitting there with an innocent face on her.

"Maybe we should have a fight after school," suggested Rachel.

"Shall I make her bark like a dog?" asked Violet telepathically.

"Please no," bellowed Lexie towards Violet.

"What, you don't want to fight me?" asked Rachel.

"I mean, yes," said Lexie addressing Rachel, but becoming quite nervous.

Rachel stared Lexie down.

"I feel like smashing your face in right now," warned Rachel indignantly.

"You need to control your feelings and emotions," Violet suggested telepathically.

"Okay," replied Lexie.

"What, you want to fight now in the library?" asked Rachel becoming a little confused with the conversation.

"No, we will fight after school," answered Lexie.

Rachel walked closer to Lexie.

"Are you scared of me now?" asked Rachel, teeth clenched with hatred.

"Would you like me to leave her alone?" said Violet telepathically.

"Yes," said Lexie.

"So you are scared of me," commented Rachel.

"No," replied Lexie.

"Make up your mind," replied Rachel sounding quite puzzled.

Violet and Nadia began to Giggle uncontrollably.

Rachel and Lexie stared each other down once again.

"See you at the showdown after school," said Rachel as she turned to leave the library.

"Shall I make her trip and fall?" asked Violet telepathically.

"Stop," shouted Lexie.

Rachel stopped in her tracks and turned back around to face her.

After a short while of playing on their mobiles, Lexie heard another message in her head coming through from Violet telepathically.

"Let's see what happens when I disconnect everyone's service from their mobiles."

"Please don't do that again," responded Lexie telepathically.

"Come on, it's the last day at school so let's have some fun," encouraged Violet.

There were some loud pings, mobiles vibrated violently and then there was silence all around.

"My mobile service has disappeared again," commented Seamus.

"Mine too," complained Nadia.

Before long everyone was grumbling and complaining.

"It's happened again," moaned Helen, "I can't cope without my mobile, I suffer from anxiety, I need my mobile to work… now!"

"What, another EMP serge?" asked Lyn.

"Yes," complained Helen, "I'll go crazy without my mobile."

"Told you, it's the end of the world," remarked Seamus.

"You talk crazy like mad Max," said Stephan.

"I heard that," said Max with an angry face, while approaching them with his friend Francisco.

"Stop playing on your mobiles and have a decent conversation with each other," suggested Violet.

Students gazed towards each other in search of a valid conclusion.

"I still think that it is to do with the electromagnetic field of Earth," suggested Helen now beginning to shake nervously with worry.

"No, I think that it is because they are installing 5G towers everywhere," said Seamus, "haven't you noticed that there are no birds flying around these days?"

Just then some birds flew over their heads. They looked up and then turned to face Seamus.

"Well, there goes your theory," giggled Lexie.

The children continued with their convoluted conspiracy theories.

The conversation began to heat up.

"My dad says they are creating Androids," said Max.

"That's not far off the truth," whispered Violet into Lexie's ear.

"What are you going on about this time?" asked Nadia.

"They are trying to create a Prototype human."

"How?" asked Lyn now becoming more interested in the conversation.

"Advanced Physicist have found some Alien DNA," replied Max.

Violet turned to face Max, now intrigued with his theories.

"So the disturbances are caused from an alien invasion?" said Debbie hysterically.

"You know that they are just turning us into mutants," said Helen.

"Isn't that from X-Men?" remarked Lexie.

Several students giggled.

"I suppose this is Alien Armageddon," commented Stephan sarcastically.

"My dad has been working on something big," replied Max indignantly.

"They are closing down schools because there is a deadly virus sweeping across our Country," suggested Seamus.

"Virus," said Debbie, "I thought you said that it was caused by 5G?"

"The Virus will kill off most of the population," continued Seamus.

"Why would they want to do that?" asked Nadia.

"We have become too overpopulated," added Seamus.

"So they have unleashed a virus on purpose?" asked Nadia anxiously.

"I hear they have already created a vaccine," said Lyn intellectually.

"I hear they are injecting them with a parasite," said Max.

"Wait, what!" screamed Lexie.

"They are injecting people with thousands of Nano mites," said Seamus.

"Don't you mean millions," interjected Stephan.

"I hear that there is a man walking around with 5 billion Nano robots in him," added Max.

"These crazy boys can't even agree on how many-."

Lexie was interrupted.

"My dad told me that the jab is laced with liquid microchips," said Stephan.

"So now they are turning us into Robots?" screamed Lyn.

Many of them chuckled with laughter, while the conversation became even more elaborate.

"Soon robots will be everywhere," said Debbie, "soon robots will be brushing our teeth for us."

"My mum brushes my teeth," commented Stephan.

"Wait, what?" said Violet.

"She says that I don't brush them properly."

Some students began to giggle uncontrollably.

The conversation went on.

"There are several reasons why some people are hesitant to take the jab," remarked Max, "In some communities, I understand, they believe that there is beef in the vaccine, in another they believe there is pork in it and in others they believe it contains aborted foetuses. I have even heard people saying it has a chip in it and it contains the Mark of the Beast. A very strong argument against the vaccine is that it was rushed out too quickly. I would argue that in nearly every sphere of life, changes are happening at a pace we can hardly keep up with. The computer or smartphone you purchased yesterday will soon become outdated."

"Interesting conclusion," said Lexie.

"Interesting my right eye," bellowed Nadia, "those are crazy conspiracy theories, I mean the vaccine contains beef and pork, how very stupid."

"Project Zion."

Violet's eyes nearly jumped out of their sockets. She then wondered if she should use her special powers to extract some information from within Max's mind.

"The military are involved," said Francisco.

"Aliens are abducting us and taking our blood," said Seamus.

"Abducted when did we get on to the subject of abduction?" asked Nadia.

"This conversation has got out of hand," said Lexie.

"I blame it on the military," said Francisco.

"I blame it on the Government," said Seamus.

"That reminds me of a famous song," said Violet with her usual mischievous smile beaming across her face.

"No, you wouldn't," said Lexie.

"Let's have some fun. Turn and face me children," Violet ordered.

In an instant, Violet had performed her mind control on them all and they all awaited a command.

"Now sing Michael Jackson blame it on the boogie, Lexie music please."

Violet's mobile began to play some music and the kids all started singing and dancing.

Don't blame it on the sunshine,

Don't blame it on the moonlight,

Don't blame it on the good times,

Blame it on the boogie.

Nadia and her girls danced with the boys, while Lexie and Violet laughed and clapped their hands whilst enjoying the entertainment.

After a short while of having fun, the school bell rang, it was the end of break.

"That was fun," said Violet while returning all the mobiles back to their normal service.

"I really wish that I had the power to do that," said Lexie.

"You do."

"How?" asked Lexie.

"You still have my magic belt on."

Just then, Max and his friend Francisco began to walk past. Violet immediately grabbed Max's hand and said, "Who does your dad work for?"

"It's a secret and I am not going to tell you."

Violet locked eyes, made the telepathic connection and then blinked.

"I need the information in your mind, don't worry you don't have to speak."

"What's going on?" asked Francisco.

Violet quickly finished downloading the information from within Max's mind.

"Max was just going to say that we should have a great day," replied Violet in an innocent tone.

"Have a great day," said Max, then he wondered off with a puzzled expression across his face.

"Did you get all the information you needed?" asked Lexie.

"Yes, but I think that I might be too late to do anything to prevent it."

"Prevent what?" asked Lexie.

"Max's dad works for a secret organisation, they have been smuggling some of the deadliest viruses into the Country."

"How are they planning to distribute the virus?"

"I don't know, but one of the traces of a virus they already have is in my DNA, it's what makes me immortal."

"So, Max's dad is trying to make someone immortal?"

"Max's dad created Dr Dre."

"Who is that?"

"He is an evil villain from my world."

"Oh, that's not good."

"He is after a special crystal Amulet from Egypt, which is an Archaeological relic, if he succeeds in finding it, then he will use it to power the virus."

"So, you need to stop him, right?"

"Yes, I need to go to Egypt right away before he causes destruction of Fathomless proportions."

"Take me with you," Lexie insisted.

"No, not this time, you need to stay and finish school."

"When will you be back?"

"I'll be back to see your fight at the end of school."

"Err, you do realise that Egypt is thousands of miles away."

"It's just a few seconds away for me."

With that, Violet gave a warm smiled and then disappeared.

Chapter 13

At the end of school, Lexie and her friend Nadia walked cautiously towards the school gate.

"Why are you walking so slowly?" asked Nadia.

"No reason," replied Lexie hesitantly, while looking all around for Rachel, who was about to take her on in a final fight.

"There's Rachel and Rebecca over there," said Nadia, "I think that she is waiting for you."

"Thanks," replied Lexie fearfully.

"You are not scared, are you?"

"She's bigger, stronger and uglier than me, so no," replied Lexie sarcastically.

"Be confident girl, you can take her."

"Where's Violet when I need her?" Lexie thought to herself, as she reluctantly stopped in front of Rachel and Rebecca.

"So you actually turned up," said Rachel, "I thought that you would chicken out."

"I'm not scared of you," replied Lexie bravely.

Students now began to encircle them, all anxious to see a fight.

"No retreat, no surrender," commented Nadia jokingly.

"No time for a joke," said Lexie nervously.

"Maybe you should surrender now before you get hurt," remarked Rachel in a sarcastic tone.

"I told you, I'm not scared of you," said Lexie as she plucked up courage to face her opponent.

"I'm gonna smash your face in," returned Rachel indignantly.

"I hope this belt is enchanted," thought Lexie adjusting the belt around her waist, hoping for good luck.

They stood close to each other and stared each other down. For a short while nothing was said, while Lexie's head swam with thought.

"Please help me God, I need Violet," thought Lexie.

Just then she heard another voice enter her head.

"I'm here, I'm right behind you."

Lexie looked over Rachel's shoulder to glance at the school gate, which was slowly changing colour. Gold, violet with a hint of blue moved swiftly through the metal bars and then Violet materialised before her.

"Do you want me to take over?" asked Violet telepathically.

"No," said Lexie.

"So, you don't want me to smash your face in?" asked Rachel.

"Don't worry, calm down and be confident," instructed Violet telepathically, "the belt you are wearing is enchanted and has powers, it will guide and protect you."

"Okay," said Lexie.

"So, you do want me to squash your face," remarked Rachel.

Lexie confidently stared into Rachel's eyes and then unknowingly blinked. She held her gaze for a few seconds making an unconscious connection.

"You hit me first," said Lexie.

"You hit me first," repeated Rachel.

"What!" remarked Lexie.

"What!" Rachel repeated with a baffled expression.

Violet began to chuckle.

Rachel wrestled within herself but was compelled to follow Lexie's commands.

There was silence as Rachel failed to speak first.

"Slap yourself in the face," instructed Lexie.

Rachel slapped herself in the face and many students laughed in hysterics.

"Holy moly, this is so cool," mumbled Lexie to herself.

Rachel stood there with a blank face.

"On your toes and bounce around with your guards up," said Lexie.

Rachel began to bounce around like a boxer and awaited another instruction.

"Shadow boxing."

Rachel threw out a few punches, ducking and weaving fast, executing some powerful jabs.

"Who does she think she is, Frank Bruno?" commented Nadia.

"Slap yourself in the face with your other hand."

Rachel slapped herself, then continued shadow boxing. Students snorted with laughter.

"What's happening to me?" Rachel asked in a confused tone.

"Ten press-ups," said Lexie.

Rachel immediately got down and began to perform press-ups, then sprang back to her feet. The crowd of students howled with laughter.

"Now begin to punch yourself in the ribs and then your face," ordered Lexie.

Rachel stood there, fighting with herself, first punching herself repeatedly in the ribs and then smacking herself in the face. There was laughter everywhere until a teacher turned up.

"That's enough fighting girls."

"I'm not fighting Sir," said Lexie confidently.

The Teacher stood there for a few seconds and observed Rachel who appeared to be fighting with herself.

"That's enough," said the Teacher.

"Stop and go home," ordered Lexie.

Rachel stopped punishing herself and then rushed off hastily, with her twin sister dashing after her. Students continued to laugh as they slowly dispersed.

Lexie walked off with Violet and Nadia with a triumphant smile beaming across her face.

"What the hell was that?" asked Nadia.

"That was fighting without fighting!" replied Lexie as Violet broke out with tears of laughter.

"I guess you won," said Violet.

"I feel invincible with this belt on," answered Lexie proudly.

"How were you controlling her actions?" asked Nadia.

Lexie then looked to Violet for an explanation of what had just happened.

"I guess your powers are evolving."

"So, am I able to control people's thoughts and actions?"

"Yep," replied Violet.

"How?" asked Nadia completely confused with the situation.

"I guess I have the power of persuasion," replied Lexie with a bright smile across her face.

They parted from Nadia outside her house and headed towards Lexie's home.

"Did you see me kicking Rachel's ass?" said Lexie.

"Technically she kicked her own ass," replied Violet jokingly.

"What else is this belt capable of?"

"Sorry to cut your fame short, but we have more important issues to deal with."

"What could be more important than controlling people's thoughts?"

"Saving the World," reminded Violet.

"Oh yes, there is that," said Lexie, "how did you get on in Egypt?"

"By the time I arrived, someone had already stolen the Amulet from Egypt."

"And you think that it was that Dr Dre?"

"Yes, but he is also going to need special DNA ,which is kept in a secret laboratory."

"How do you know this?"

"I extracted the information from within Max's mind. His father is an advanced Physicist and working on something called Project Zion. They have created a Bio-weapon and they are going to unleash it. Many people are focussed on destroying the Earth and they are planning to bring the world to its knees."

"What's that got to do with the virus?"

"The virus is just a part of it. They have hidden agendas and we have to protect our species."

"So, what now?"

"I'm afraid I'm gonna have to leave again."

Lexie stopped outside her house and turned to face Violet.

"Take me with you?" Lexie insisted.

"We need to make an intercontinental trip."

"Where?"

"America."

Lexie looked as though she was about to suffer from travel sickness.

"So… are you ready for your next mission?"

With that they both teleported and vanished, reappearing seconds later in America.

Chapter 14

The bright light slowly dissipated as they glided to a stop. Distorted images slowly became in focus. Violet consulted her mobile, while Lexie glanced around to observe their surroundings.

"Where are we?" asked Lexie.

"We should be just outside UCLA University in Los Angeles."

"This is the 12th best university in the world," informed Lexie, "situated near Beverly Hills and that's an awful lot of steps."

Lexie slowly looked up towards the top.

"Eighty-seven I believe," commented Violet.

"It looks deserted, where is everyone?"

"Schools and colleges have all closed last week due to the virus spreading all over the world."

"So why are we here?"

"Dr Dre will need something from the science lab in the south campus, but first I need to get changed into my combat clothes."

Lexie had a quick look at what she was wearing.

"And what about me, I'm still in my school clothes?"

Violet glanced at her mobile and muttered, "Lexie."

In a flash both their clothes changed into army type outfits.

"Going blond today," said Lexie.

"I thought that I would appear as myself," replied Violet, "I'm afraid it could get a little messy this time."

They slowly began to ascend the steps.

Outside the entrance there were two guards with guns.

"Dr Dre must already be here," said Violet, "we are going to need to get past those guards. Are you ready?"

"To what, run? They have guns."

"You take the one on the left and I will take the one on the right."

"Wait… what!" said Lexie fearfully.

"Use your mind control to compel him to drop his gun."

Lexie looked at Violet with a blank face.

"Don't worry, you are still wearing my enchanted belt."

"Holy, moly," Lexie gulped as they both walked towards the guards.

"Hi, could you help me?" asked Violet confidently.

Both the guards turned their heads and looked down towards the girls.

"This campus is closed," stated one of the guards.

That's all it took for both the girls to make eye contact and they telepathically compelled the guards to drop their guns and fall asleep.

"Holy, moly it worked," screeched Lexie triumphantly, "my powers must be getting even stronger, because I never spoke out verbally."

"Let's go this way, follow me," ordered Violet.

Lexie looked into the distance at the vast amount of space.

"This University is huge."

"It's over 400 acres I believe," said Violet.

They walked past a water fountain and a huge statue of a bear.

After a short while they came across another building guarded by several gunmen.

"Are you ready?" Violet asked.

"I was born ready," replied Lexie.

"Put on your sunglasses," a female voice shouted from a distance.

The three guards reached into their pockets hastily and placed sunglasses on their faces.

"We are unable to make eye contact," said Violet Shakely, "They must know we are here."

"Shall we run?" Lexie asked in a panic.

"No, stand behind me."

Violet approached the men with Lexie closely behind, so as not in the line of fire. She then spoke to her mobile just as the three men broke out in gun fire.

"This is scary," shouted Lexie.

The bullets seemed to bounce off Violet's body like pin pong balls. When she was close enough she wrestled with the three men, kicking and punching them until they dropped the guns and were out cold on the floor. One of them moved around as though he was about to restore himself to his feet. Violet reached out and snatched his sunglasses from his face.

"Now stay down and sleep." Commanded Violet.

"Oh my God," muttered Lexie, "my twin is a bad ass fighter."

"It's clear, let's go," ordered Violet, while walking away.

"I thought that you couldn't fight?" Lexie asked.

"I never said that I couldn't fight, I said that I do not like fighting," replied Violet.

"How were you able to Repel the bullets?"

"I guess my skin is tough."

"My twin is a superhero," mumbled Lexie as they walked around the next corner.

"Three more with weapons this time and all wearing sunglasses. Wait here."

Violet dashed off while Lexie observed the battle. Violet blocked manoeuvred and managed to overcome all three in a matter of seconds.

"I thought that I saw one of them stab you," remarked Lexie.

"I can withstand blows from a sword or stab from a speer."

"Holy moly, she is invincible," thought Lexie.

"How did they know to wear sunglasses and who was that girl?" muttered Violet.

"Should we call the cops?" advised Lexie.

"They are on the way," replied Violet.

They walked on and ahead they saw about five criminals wearing sunglasses.

"There's too many, I don't think that I can stop them all."

"So... should we run now?" gestured Lexie.

"You are going to have to help me."

"But I can't fight," remarked Lexie.

"Do you trust me??" Violet asked.

"Yes."

"Then look into my eyes."

Lexie looked towards Violet an she stared back at her. They stood there for a few seconds before Lexie staggered backwards.

"Are you okay?" Violet asked with concern.

There was a short pause before Lexie answered saying,

"I think I know Kung Fu."

Violet smiled.

"How is that possible?" Lexie asked.

"I uploaded a Martial Arts manual into your brain."

"Cool," responded Lexie.

"Now… let's test it out on them," said Violet in a more serious tone.

They headed over and began to fight and defend themselves. Violet, with her super quick reflexes took most of them, but Lexie managed to knock one of them down with a jump spinning heel kick to his head.

"Holy, moly, where did that come from?"

"I guess you really do know Kung-Fu," replied Violet cheerfully.

There headed through the entrance and walked towards the secret lab, only to encounter several more thugs.

"Three men with guns guarding that door and we need to get through," exclaimed Violet.

"Okay, okay," hesitated Lexie, "you disarm them and I'll kick their ass."

"Sounds like a plan, let's go," replied Violet as she hurried forwards.

The men were prepared and all had their sunglasses on, so Violet had to fight through a round of gunfire before disarming them and leaving Lexie to finish them off.

"Now that's team work," bellowed Lexie triumphantly as the last man fell to the ground and remained unconscious.

Violet turned the handle and slowly opened the door. Before them stood over twenty gunmen armed and dangerous.

"Get behind me quick," shouted Violet, just as they opened with gunfire.

"Stop firing," a female voice ordered, "your petty guns are no match for her."

The gunfire stopped and they all stood awaiting another command. Violet and the girl stared at each other as though they recognised one another.

"Who is she?" asked Lexie.

Chapter 15

A moment passed before they spoke.

"Hello again Violet."

"Asha-D, what are you doing here?"

Before them stood a tall teenage girl with long brown hair and hazel eyes.

"You know her?" asked Lexie in a raised tone.

"Yes," replied Violet, "she's from my World."

"You mean she's from the future? I thought that we were looking for Dr Dre?" asked Lexie.

"Asha is his accomplice, why are you here?" Violet directed towards Asha-D, while glancing around the room to see two Doctors bound and gagged.

"Changing the future," replied Asha with a smug smile.

"And what do you plan to do with them?" asked Violet pointing towards the captive Scientists.

"I am changing the course of history by having the serum for myself," replied Asha while holding up a vile, "this vile contains the secret of your powers... and now it's mine."

Asha-D laughed.

"You will destroy the humans," remarked Violet.

"We need to evolve," commented Asha, "So it will be a new beginning and science requires sacrifice."

Lexie focussed on the two captive Scientists.

"They look like the doctors that performed the surgery on my kidney," remarked Lexie, "what have they got to do with it?"

"They conjured the serum from your blood platelets," replied Asha now looking directly towards Lexie, "and they cloned your DNA."

"What's that got to do with me?" Lexie asked innocently.

"Hasn't Violet told you?" asked Asha, "you are the key to project Zion."

Lexie turned her head to face Violet awaiting an explanation.

There was a slight hesitation before Violet chose to speak. "I surgically inserted a new kidney into you using my blood," explained Violet, "unfortunately the Doctors realised that my blood was alien, so they have been secretly developing it here, in this lab."

Lexie was left speechless, baffled with the information she had just learnt.

"And now it's all mine," screeched Asha-D.

"I'll stop you," said Violet.

Asha laughed then said, "You're too late."

"What are you going to do with the serum?" asked Violet in a concerned tone.

"Change history and bring the World to their knees," bellowed Asha, "with just one dose I can create more people to think like me."

"You're sick," said Violet.

"I thought you said only boys were bad!" Lexie commented.

"She must be damaged, but I don't understand why… and now I have to stop her."

Two gunmen prepare to fire, but Asha-Dee raised a hand and shouted, "Stop."

Lexie moved her foot and stood behind Violet out of the line of fire.

"We have to protect our species," said Violet while staring directly into Asha D's eyes.

She stared and blinked to make the telepathic connection.

"Something wrong?" asked Asha Dee with a victorious smile now beaming across her face.

"Why isn't this working?" Violet whispered into Lexie's ear.

"Use your telekinesis," muttered Lexie.

"I'm trying, I can't control her thoughts."

"But she's not wearing sunglasses," said Lexie.

"Would you like me to come a little closer so that you can make a better connection?" asked Asha with confidence, while walking slowly closer.

They were now stood inches away from each other. Asha was about 5' 10" and towered over Violet, who was about 5 foot 5.

They stared for a few seconds. into each other's eyes but nothing happened. Violet tried once more to use her mind control on her but failed to make any connection.

"How?" asked Violet.

"I had a feeling I would run into one of you telepaths, I have developed a powerful new secret weapon, so you are unable to read my mind."

"Why are you doing this?"

"Power is power."

"I'll stop you."

"Your powers are no match for me," returned Asha-D, boastfully.

Violet performed a strike towards her face, but Asha-D blocked it with ease. They exchanged blows, while Lexie stood back. Asha was able to counter Violets super quick strikes and soon knocked her to the ground.

"Oh my God," screamed Lexie with both her hands in front of her mouth.

"Stay back," ordered Violet while quickly returning to her feet.

The fight restarted and they exchanged a few more blows, kicking and punching each other before Violet was knocked down once more.

Lexie ran over and crouched down on her knees near to Violet. "Come on, another round," she encouraged.

"Maybe you should take her on," suggested Violet.

Lexie looked up and faced Asha-Dee who was just standing there, looking tall, mean and waiting for more.

"My powers have not evolved enough yet so maybe you should keep fighting her."

"You're a great help," remarked Violet.

"No retreat, no surrender remember," advised Lexie.

"Yeah, yeah," muttered Violet as she reluctantly faced her opponent.

A few more seconds passed, while they exchanged blows. They blocked and countered each other until Violet was violently thrown to the floor once more.

"We need help, we need reinforcement," advised Lexie hysterically.

Asha walked over to Violet. She looked down at her and began to gloat. Violet slowly returned to her feet and groaned in pain. Asha-D began to assist Violet by holding her shoulder steady with one arm.

"You're finished," bellowed Asha-D, "you held the future of the entire World in your hands, I am here to take it back."

Asha-D quickly reached into her leather belt and pulled out a dagger. She lunged her other arm forwards and plunged it deep into Violet's chest saying, "Martial Arts is built on deception."

"No," screamed Lexie while dashing over to her aid.

Violet fell into Lexie's arms and they both looked down at her injury. The dagger had somehow pierced her unbreakable skin and she was wounded badly.

"How?" muttered Violet who was bleeding and now too weak to fight on.

"I thought that I might encounter you, so I brought it from the future."

Lexie began to cry. Tears streamed down her face as Violet drew ever weaker.

"Today I lose a sister," said Asha-D, while staring down at Violet's dying body.

"Police, don't move," a commanding voice shouted.

Just then there was gunfire. Lexie turned her head around to see several Cops entering the room.

"Kill them, kill them all," Asha commanded pointing towards the Cops.

They exchanged gunfire with the thugs, killing some but not able to penetrate Asha-Dee's skin. She repelled the bullets as she made her escape.

"Asha-D, has an invisible force field and able to selfheal, so I am gonna call for help using my telekinesis," whispered Violet weakly, while glancing towards her mobile.

Lexie carefully observed Asha-D's countenance as she made her getaway.

"She's got a leather belt on similar to your belt that I am wearing," commented Lexie, "if you wear mine will it help you heal too?"

"Yes, but you need it for protection, if you take it off, you will be left vulnerable."

Lexie looked towards her dying twin sister, who was bleeding severely from her tummy.

"I'm not ready to lose a sister."

With that, Lexie removed the belt from around her waist and placed it around Violet.

"Please don't die," pleaded Lexie.

"Be strong, don't be afraid because I am healed," responded Violet.

Her wounds began to close up rapidly as her cells slowly regenerated.

"I'm healed," repeated Violet.

Lexie looked as the last part of her wound disappeared. Within seconds Violet sprang back to her feet.

"How is that possible?"

"My DNA has been altered so wounds don't last, they just regenerate."

"It really was you in the hospital that told me not to be afraid, wasn't it?"

"Yes, but you're gonna have to stay here, out of harm's way," ordered Violet.

Lexie gave a warm smile. "Go kick her ass," she said in encouragement, just as Violet casually levitated and then disappeared.

Outside, Asha was just about to escape in a car with the two captive Doctors, when Violet descended upon her with an airborne kick, knocking her to the ground. Asha jumped back to her feet and said, "How were you able to regenerate?"

"I guess I have a few secrets too," remarked Violet, "my father upgraded my belt."

"That belt won't save you, you are no match for me," returned Asha while floating over to Violet to resume their fight.

"Bring it on bitch!" said Violet.

They kicked and punched, blocking and countering each other's strikes. Violet, with her super quick reflexes managed to block and counter at the same time, knocking Asha to the ground a few times.

"It's all over," said Violet, this time looking down towards Asha.

"Shoot her," Asha ordered in desperation.

Asha directed two gunmen to open fire on her, while instructing her mobile to shoot a ray onto a building. It collapsed onto Violet and she was buried deep beneath the rubble. Asha became overconfident and decided to enter the other building to finish off Lexie.

There was gunfire in the distance when Lexie saw Violet re-enter the room looking mysteriously calm.

"Did you manage to finish off Asha?" asked Lexie.

"Yes," replied Violet with a crooked smile.

Violet slowly walked over to Lexie and stopped directly in front of her.

"So what now?" asked Lexie.

There was a pause before Violet spoke, "Unfortunately, I am going to have to kill you too."

"What?"

"You have nobody here to help you."

"She's got me, her sister from another Mister," another voice shouted.

They both turned their heads to see another Violet standing in the doorway.

"What's happening?" Lexie asked nervously while glancing towards both Violets, "I'm freaking out over here."

"That's Asha, she's a replicator," warned the real Violet, "Asha's taken on my physical form.

Asha began to reach into her belt to retrieve her dagger. Just then, there was the sound of thunder coming from outside. They all turned to peer out of the window. In the sky was a rainbow that appeared to be growing at lightning speed. Red, yellow and blue swept through the sky and entered the room. The red image kicked

Asha away from Lexie and then materialised. Standing next to Lexie was now another girl, dressed in a red hooded cloak.

"Someone call for help?" asked the girl in red, speaking with a Russian accent.

"Yes," replied Violet.

With a groan, the other Violet slowly rearrange her image to appear as Asha-D.

"How did you know which Violet was the real one?" Lexie enquired.

"That's easy," replied the girl cheekily, "I could smell her.

They laughed.

"This is my friend Roxie Redding," said Violet.

"People call me Red," the girl corrected.

"I can see why," said Lexie.

Red had, well, long red hair and a long red cloak. She was wearing a similar belt that was red and white with blue crystals, fastened together with a two headed eagle.

Besided Violet now stood four more girls in brilliant bright colours. They all looked like teenage girls, maybe thirteen to eighteen years old and all looking ready for a fight.

"And who are they?" asked Lexie.

"Standing next to me is Gloria dressed in yellow, Helen in red, white and blue, India in Green and Tamir Taylour in red."

"People call me Mr T," added Tamia, who was a tall, toned girl, with green eyes and long black braided hair down to her waist.

"Have you all forgotten about me?" asked Asha-D.

Red casually turned her head to glance over her shoulder.

"Don't be rude, nobody's speaking to you."

Asha sighed deeply. Red then turned her head to face Lexie and continued to ignore her. "I've brought this along for you as instructed."

Red pulled out a belt from her pocket. It was a gold belt with gemstones of every colour of the rainbow, fastened together with two red lions.

"For me?" asked Lexie in excitement.

Red placed the belt around Lexie's waist and fastened it tightly. The Amber crystal on the belt immediately lit up.

"Now you're one of us," said Red.

"The Rainbow girls are now complete," added Tamir.

Lexie had an immediate head rush and then staggered backwards.

"What was that?" asked Lexie.

"That is your new powers rushing through your body," replied Red.

"I feel like my mind has switched from analogue to digital," said Lexie in excitement.

"Ladies, we have a situation," interrupted Violet.

All the girls, including Red, reached into their belts and produced their own styles of weaponry. Red pulled out a spear, Helen produced a handful of white darts shaped like stars, Gloria magically produced a long wooden staff out of her red belt, India reached into her green and white belt and had a handful of small blue wheels and Tamir pulled out of her red, green and yellow belt a pair of golden boxing gloves.

"Dr Dre is here."

"How did he manage to get from our World?" asked Helen, looking toned and flexible and nothing like Helen from school, who was quite timid.

"He must have travelled through the portal," continued Violet, "he's somewhere here on the UCLA campus."

"I can smell him," said Red, "he's close so we will go and seek him out."

With that, they all vanished and joined the Cops fighting the criminals outside.

"Where is Dr Dre?" asked Violet addressing Asha.

"You are all mistaken, I travelled here alone."

"Tell me where he is, or I'll beat it out of you."

Asha stared towards her and said, "You do not possess the power to finish me off."

Violet began to walk past Lexie. Just as she drew level with her, Lexie extended her left arm in front of Violet's chest to stop her.

"Let me take this one on," suggested Lexie.

"You have only just come into your powers, maybe you're not ready."

"Let me test out my powers?" asked Lexie.

"Okay, your powers are tethered to the belt. The belt follows your thoughts, so believe in your abilities and you will succeed."

Chapter 16

Lexie turned her head towards Asha-D and spoke.

"This is your last chance, where is Dr Dre?"

Asha-D laughed and said, "What can a mere mortal do to me?"

Violet stood back and Lexie slowly approached Asha, until they were standing toe to toe. Asha-D was about 6 inches taller than Lexie, so looked down to her and confidently smiled.

Outside, the teenage girls were taking on the gunmen. Red spoke out and said, "Guns."

The guns from three gunmen flew out of their hands and high into the air, before landing by her feet. India spun around and knocked one down with a single kick, while Red ran forwards to finish the other two off with some jump kicks. Helen swung her long golden hair and they appeared to have a mind of their own. Magical strands of her hair flew into the sky and hovered over the thugs. They then swooped down, twisted and bound several men while she lunged forwards to finish them off with a selection of aerodynamic kicks.

Back inside, Violet spoke out and said, "No retreat, no surrender."

Lexie turned her head to take a quick glance over her shoulder towards Violet. Just as she gave her a smile, Asha kicked her in the chest, knocking her across the floor. Lexie was quick to get back on her feet. Asha approached and the fight began. A few seconds past and Lexie was able to overpower Asha kicking her to the floor with a spinning heel kick. She was back up and fighting back hard, but Lexie seemed to be able to block everything and eventually punched her to the ground.

"What is this," shouted Asha in frustration.

"That was just 50% of my skills," said Lexie, "now here's 60%."

Lexie lunged forwards. Using Wing-Chun, her arms were quicker, blocking and countering Asha until she went down. Asha was bruised but it soon faded. She wiped off some blood from her lips with a hand. Lexie lashed out and gave her a slap in the face.

"What was that for?" asked Asha in total surprise while rubbing her bruised check.

"I thought that I would bitch slap you back to the future!"

"Well, it never worked, so what's next?"

"Here's 70% of my skills," answered Lexie.

They fought on, both kicking and punching, blocking and countering strikes. Asha tried to catch Lexie's foot, but she anticipated her move and after landing a kick near her shoulder, Lexie spun around and executed a jump back kick with her other foot, connecting with Asha's chin. Asha was down again and now desperate for assistance.

Outside, Red had called several times for guns, making them fly out of the criminal's hands. Then she disarmed several of them with her spear. Tamir ran and grabbed two of their heads and smashed them together, knocking them both out in an instant. She then had a boxing fight with one that didn't last very long before she gave him a hard right hook. Tamir then grabbed another one, lifting him up and just throwing him into the water fountain like he was a tennis ball. Then she grabbed two of them in the midst of them punching and kicking and placed them in front of two Officers that had joined them. The Officers handcuffed them, baffled with confusion on how this teenage girl was able to handle herself with such ease.

Lexie stared towards Asha who had just been knocked down.

"Now here's 80%."

They fought on, kicking and punching, blocking and striking until Asha had space to do a run up. She ran towards Lexie and executed a flying side kick towards Lexie's head. Lexie's lightning reflexes were too quick and she literally caught Asha's leg in mid-flight, causing her to fall to the ground. Asha-D was back up and fought on. Lexie was in with hands moving at lightning speed. Asha staggered back giving Lexie space to have a slight run up. She ran forwards, performing a triple jump front kick to her chest. Then Lexie executed a jump roundhouse to her jaw. Asha was down and now hurt quite badly, but the bruises magically faded once more. Asha-D slowly returned to her feet and groaned in pain.

Lexie took one final look at Asha-D and said, "And now my full 100%."

Violet watched as Lexie continued to batter Asha. With her super quick reflexes, she was able to dodge and strike Asha, wounding her some more. Her moves were now so fast that Asha positively appeared slow. Lexie's techniques were so quick that her hands and legs moved almost instinctively bordering precognition. She blocked some strikes from Asha, and gave her a shower of punches to her chest, then she turned around to perform a jump back kick. Asha flew across the room and fell to the ground in pain. She walked over to Asha and placed her hands around her neck. Lexie began to choke her to death.

"Where's the Doctor?" Lexie screamed while shaking her violently.

Asha sounded like she was choking. Violet watched from a distance and saw Asha's countenance changing. Asha's image melted away to rearrange itself and she slowly materialise as... Dr Dre.

"Watch out," Violet screamed.

Lexie quickly manoeuvred out of the way of a dirty punch and stood to her feet.

Both Violet and Lexie stood looking at him. All the wounds had regenerated and healed rapidly.

"Who are you?" Lexie asked.

"Don't you already know?" he replied, "I'm Dr Dre."

"No, you're a dead beat," interjected Violet.

"Dressing up as a girl, that's an all-time low," commented Lexie.

"Wearing your girly perfume was the only way to cover up my smell, so that I could go about undetected."

Dr Dre laughed.

"Why have you really travelled back through the portal?" asked Violet.

"To change history, I now possess the power. I can create a new World order, led by me."

"They won't follow you, you're crazy," said Violet, "you're just a twisted psychopath."

"They will have no choice, unless we alter their minds, there will be no future for the human race because they will destroy themselves, so I have unleashed a poisonous gas into their atmosphere and my virus is now airborne. If they don't take my vaccine then they will all die."

Dr Dre cackled nastily.

"Why would you want to do that?" asked Lexie.

"Because the weak don't deserve to inherit the Earth, no, only the strong will survive," he snapped back.

"So, you only want criminals in the future?" asked Violet.

"No, no," added Dr Dre shaking his head violently, "criminals and druggies are paranoid, so they won't take the vaccine. They are too sceptical and untrustworthy to lead my empire. Those crooks would rob their own mother! They are so convinced that one of their conspiracy theories are correct that they don't realise they are all slowly been poisoned. Those who choose to wear the masks will live, while all the others will surely… die."

"That will leave an unspeakable trail of human carnage," said Lexie.

"I won't let you go through with it," added Violet.

"You don't have the power to stop me," he cackled, "you fool, you can't win, I have already succeeded. Some of my men have escaped with your captive Scientists. The world around us is changing and evolving, evil wins."

"It's time to end this perpetual battle between good and evil," suggested Violet.

"I am just trying to save our race," he replied in mild indignation.

"You had a twisted sense of saving the World," remarked Violet.

"You are insane," said Lexie.

"Thank you," replied Dr Dre in a condescending tone.

"But innocent people will die," said Violet.

"Death is what causes people to live. I am changing the course of history. Either they have the jab… or die."

He cackled with laughter.

Outside, Gloria levitated and was flying around knocking into thugs similar to knocking down skittles.

"Strike," she shouted as another ten bad guys fell to the ground.

Tamir then dragged them like human puppets into the arms of Cops to be arrested. Gloria stood in front of one guy and looked up. He was much taller than her. She jumped up and executed a 360 degree spinning kick that went over his head. He laughed thinking that she had missed. She then punched him between the legs and he went down groaning. Helen threw a few white stars and they knocked guns out of the bad guy's hands. She then kicked off their sun glasses, made eye contact and said, "Go to sleep."

They fell to the ground unconscious. India threw her blue wheels high into the air. They grew like giant rubber tyres and then descended over bad guys heads down towards their bodies. The wheels then tightened firmly around their torso. The criminals were trapped. Cops with puzzled faces made their arrests. Red zapped several gunmen with her X-Ray eyes as more Cops came to save the day. Red then stood next to Helen.

"I have just felt a stronger sent," said Red looking back towards the building containing Violet and Lexie.

"Where is Dr Dre?" asked Helen striking another thug with a backfist to his face, as he approached her from the rear.

"Dr Dre is back inside with Lexie."

Chapter 17

Violet slowly approached Dr Dre and said, "Don't you know how dangerous it is messing with time? Who knows what kind of history we have to go back to. If you do that, there will be whole generations lost."

"It's too late to stop me, you're all too late."

"He's crazy," added Lexie while drawing level with Violet.

"My men have already escaped with my jet fuel for my fleet of fighters. The future… is mine."

"We will put an end to your quest," said Lexie bravely.

He gazed into her eyes. "You're nothing but a rug rat, not even old enough to possess any real powers."

"We can do this the easy way or the hard way."

"What's the hard way?"

"We kick your ass."

There was a short pause before he suddenly swung at Lexie. She dodged out of the way and countered with some punches. Violet joined in and attacked him from the rear, while Lexie continued to attack from the front. He was outmatched as Lexie caught him with a right hook and he soon went down. He was quickly back up fighting for his life. Lexie performed a series of blocks before executing a 360 degree kick to his head. He staggered as Violet came and hit him with a flying side kick to the other side of his head. He flew across the room and fell to the ground hard groaning in pain.

"You're finished," said Lexie.

He stood up and quickly reached into his belt with both hands. He thrust forwards with a silver sword in each hand, missing Lexie as she summersaulted out of the way landing back on her feet.

"He's got two swords," Violet informed.

"What else have you got under that belt?" Lexie asked.

"See if you are quick enough to dodge these, little girl," He remarked.

Lexie paused in thought and then reached into her gold belt producing a pair of red glowing Nunchucks, wooden sticks held together with a short chain. She spun it around her body a few times, ending with it under her armpit.

"What!" He shouted in shock.

She reached into her belt once more and produced another set of white glowing nunchucks. She spun them both around her body, before striking him in the jaw with one.

"Impressive," encouraged Violet.

Dr Dre and Lexie proceeded to dodge and strike out at each other, until Lexie knocked one of the swords out of his hand with one of her Nunchucks.

"One down, one to go," said Lexie while swinging and twisting her Nunchucks around. She speeded up so he could hardly see the sticks. You could hear the Nunchucks whistling through the air. Before he could blink she executed a strike and the other sword flew out of his other hand.

Dr Dre stood there not sure what to do. He watched as the red and white light omitting from the Nunchucks became dazzling. Lexie then spun both Nunchucks around a few times at an alarming speed before striking him hard into his jaw. It crushed his face. He went down and turned his head towards Lexie. His face was contorted, damaged badly, but once again his cells regenerated. He stood up and said, "You can't beat me, I can self-heal after your every strike."

He reached back into his belt and produced a Positron gun.

"Look out," Violet screamed.

A flash of red entered the room and quickly stood in the line of fire. Roxie had her invisible force field up, which took and absorbed the blow from the ray. The other teenage girls flew in swiftly and surrounded Dr Dre.

"Shields up," Red commanded.

The other girls, including Violet put their Electromagnetic force fields up. They then began to jump, twist and fly in every direction, hoping to divert his attention from Lexie, who was vulnerable and unaware of her other gifts.

He shot, missing Gloria as she knocked him to the ground with a flying side kick.

"Strike," she bellowed victoriously.

Magical strands of Helen's hair glided towards him and tied him in a knot. He gave a nasty smile as they were unable to fasten tightly. They slowly uncoiled and fell to the ground. He then fired at her, but her force field left her unharmed. He stood up and turned to face India. She dodged around, managing to turn his back towards Lexie. She threw a selection of blue wheels into the air and they descended down on him, tightening hard, but then ascending back into the air and whisked back into India's white belt. He smiled nastily and fired, but her force field repelled the energy blast. Dr Dre growled with fury, while Violet spoke to Lexie.

"You need to get out of here, that Positron gun is from the future and can kill you."

"I'm not leaving you," replied Lexie.

"Chair," called Red.

A chair glided into her arms. She then quickly smashed it over his head and he collapsed to the ground in pain. The bruises faded just as he got back to his feet. Red shot some X-Rays from her eyes towards him. There was the sound of an explosion as the room lit up. When the dust settled, Dr Dre was still left standing and laughing nastily towards her.

"I am invincible," he shouted in triumph.

"His force field is impenetrable," advised Red just as he hit her with another blast from his Positron gun.

"Try me," bellowed Tamir running in to grab him. She showered him with some punches, using her boxing gloves. She battered him. She then rammed his head off the wall several times before leaving him in a pile on the floor. He staggered to his feet clumsily. She then held him over her head before throwing him hard against the wall once more. He groaned in pain as his wounds quickly healed. He then fired towards Tamir.

"I am immortal, none of you possess enough power to destroy me," he boasted.

"His force field is impenetrable," shouted Violet just as he turned to face her.

He laughed nastily before firing. Violet's force field was fortunately able to withstand the blast. He then slowly turned and looked directly into Lexie's eyes.

They gazed at each other for a second as the tension grew.

"You're mine now," he warned, "serve us or perish."

He walks forwards. Lexie hears a voice from Violet using her telepathy saying,

"Believe in your abilities."

Lexie drops both her red and white Nunchucks and slowly begins to levitate.

"This is your last chance to abandon your quest," advised Lexie.

"Nobody can stop me," he remarked.

"Your actions have consequences," warned Lexie.

"I will finish what I started," he ordered furiously.

Lexie gazed directly into his eyes and said, "Not today."

He fired towards Lexie. She glowed brightly. All the colours of the rainbow appeared, as the seven different gemstones on her gold belt lit up. She then glowed a brilliant white. There was tension in the room before she responded. Her Electromagnetic force field absorbed all the energy from the blast and held onto it, awaiting a command. She then extended her left arm towards him to release the energy. The energy which Dr Dre had fired towards her then flowed through her arm and sent a blast directly back towards him. There was a loud bang and a slight scream, before he was obliterated and disappeared into a billion particles.

Violet and the other teenage girls looked towards Lexie, who was still floating and then they glanced over towards where Dr Dre was standing. He had gone, vanished, at long last destroyed. For a second there was silence, before they all broke-out with an explosion of cheering. Violet floated over to Lexie and then they glided down to the ground.

"You did it," she smiled.

The others swiftly joined them with a group hug.

"That's my girl," said Red.

"Now that's girl power," said Tamir with a cheerful smile.

"Who runs the World now, you shmuck?" Violet raised.

"Girls!" they all replied.

There was a warm sound of laughter echoing around the room.

The teenage girls still glanced around in amazement.

"How did you manage to vanquish him?" Helen asked.

"I believed that I had the power to destroy him," said Lexie proudly, "some of your powers transferred into me, I then combined all of your powers, amplifying mine seven fold."

"I pity the fool," commented Tamir.

They all giggled with laughter.

"You possess extraordinary powers," remarked Red.

"What's the extent of your powers?" added India.

"I don't know yet," answered Lexie while gently stroking her gold belt, with a bright smile beaming across her face.

"How did you manage to conjure power without a special mobile?" asked Violet.

"I guess my powers are evolving so we probably won't need mobiles in the future."

"You are gifted beyond belief," commented Gloria, "knock them dead."

They laughed some more.

Lexie moved in closer to Violet and said, "Is it really all over?"

"No, the battle has just begun," replied Violet, "some of Dr Dre's men got away and are still focussed on destroying the Earth. He altered time and now we have to put the World back to normal. It's imperative that we go back."

"What! You're leaving so soon?" asked Lexie becoming slightly tearful.

The other girls moved in closer.

"It is about balance, light and dark balance must be restored," said Red.

"Peace must be restored," continued Violet, "we are in a path of destruction. The cosmic powers have already been thrown off balance. Who knows what kind of history we have to go back to."

"Dr Dre unleashed poisonous gas, so what about us, will you leave us to all die?" Lexie asked becoming slightly anxious.

"In the future, we have the technology to create a new vaccine quickly."

"So, you will come back to save us?"

"Yes, you're one of us now," said India.

"We are so proud of you, and you were very brave and strong," added Tamir.

"Lexie, you saved us," said Gloria.

"You are all saviours of the world," returned Lexie.

"No, you are," replied Violet, "you are my little sister."

"We are made from the same DNA as Violet, so that makes you our little sister too," informed Red.

"Wait, what?" asked Lexie.

"We are all made from your DNA," commented Helen.

"So, they are my twins too?" asked Lexie while slowly turning to face Violet.

"Yes."

"But… they all look so… different," commented Lexie glancing towards each teenage girl.

"Our DNA are from your blood platelets," said India, "how we turn out is nothing to do with our blood or nationality, it is based on our abilities to make better choices in life."

"You now possess an array of gifts, use them wisely," advised Gloria.

Lexie began to hug them all in excitement.

"Dr Dre is dead," said Violet while embracing Lexie, "you have nothing to be worried about anymore."

"Are you sure his tissues can't regenerate?" asked Lexie.

"You destroyed him," commented Violet, "he's gone, who runs the World now?"

"Girls," they all shouted in unison.

They then broke out in song.

After a short moment of enjoying themselves, they turned to Lexie.

"The wheels of time are against us, so we are going to have to leave and return while the portal is still open," suggested Red.

"We are going too." said the others.

Lexie hung her head down in disappointment.

"Don't worry," said Red, "you're one of the Rainbow girls now."

"What do you mean?"

"You complete the seven colours of the rainbow," said India who was wearing a green, white and indigo belt."

"I'm wearing red, white and blue," said Helen showing off her stars and stripes.

"Your middle name is Amber, which is the same as orange," said Gloria whilst clutching her red and yellow belt.

"That's just a weird coincidence," said Lexie.

"See, you were destined to join us," said Tamir who was wearing a red, green and gold belt.

"You complete our Rainbow, but I'm afraid we have to leave," said Red.

The teenage girls all walked over to Lexie. Red extended her left arm to reveal her mobile phone. She then said,

"Lexie, take us home."

Her mobile lit up and flashed a series of dazzling colours. They gave Lexie a last group hug and then disappeared in a warm swift breeze, leaving only Violet to say her goodbyes.

"Sorry, but I am going to have to join them too," said Violet while taking a last look out of a window at the beautiful rainbow that had just appeared in the sky.

"Please don't leave me here all alone," replied Lexie becoming slightly emotional.

"You need to control your feelings and emotions, that's our first discipline."

"Okay, but I have superpowers now so I can go with you, please let me come, please… please?" Lexie pleaded.

BV - #0014 - 280922 - C0 - 210/148/8 - PB - 9781913839710 - Gloss Lamination